THE PENGUIN POETS
COLLECTED POEMS

James Joyce was born in Dublin on 2 February 1882.
He was one of a large family described by his father as
"sixteen or seventeen children." He was educated at
Clongowes Wood College and later at Belvedere College, Dublin. He did well at school, being interested in
poetry, Latin, and languages. In 1898 he went to the
Dublin college of the Royal University, where he
studied philosophy and languages. He was interested
in the theatre and in April 1900 wrote in the *Fort-
nightly Review* on Ibsen's *When We Dead Awaken*.
In October 1902 Joyce went to Paris, but returned to
Dublin in 1903, as his mother was dying. He taught at
a school in Dalkey until he married in 1904, when he
and his wife went to Zürich and later Trieste, where
Joyce taught languages in the Berlitz school.

He returned to Dublin in 1912, when he made an
unsuccessful attempt to publish *Dubliners* privately.
He spent the First World War in Zürich with his wife
and two children in great poverty, but was helped by a
grant of £100 from the Privy Purse. He lived in Paris
from 1920, and published in 1922 *Ulysses* and in 1939
Finnegans Wake. He died in January 1941.

MAJOR WORKS
BY
JAMES JOYCE

FICTION
*Dubliners
*A Portrait of the Artist as a Young Man
*Ulysses
*Finnegans Wake
*Stephen Hero

POETRY
*Chamber Music
*Pomes Penyeach

OTHER WORKS
*Exiles *(play)*
Giacomo Joyce *(notebook)*

COLLECTIONS
*Collected Poems
Letters of James Joyce *(three volumes)*
*The Critical Writings of James Joyce
*Selected Letters
*The Portable James Joyce

CRITICAL LIBRARY EDITIONS
*A Portrait of the Artist as a Young Man
(edited by Chester G. Anderson)
*Dubliners *(edited by Robert Scholes and A. Walton Litz)*

Available in paperback.

COLLECTED POEMS

JAMES JOYCE

PENGUIN BOOKS

Penguin Books Ltd, Harmondsworth,
Middlesex, England
Penguin Books, 40 West 23rd Street,
New York, New York 10010, U.S.A.
Penguin Books Australia Ltd, Ringwood,
Victoria, Australia
Penguin Books Canada Limited, 2801 John Street,
Markham, Ontario, Canada L3R 1B4
Penguin Books (N.Z.) Ltd, 182–190 Wairau Road,
Auckland 10, New Zealand

Published in a Viking Compass Edition
in the United States of America 1957
Reprinted 1959, 1960,
1961, 1963, 1964, 1966, 1967, 1968,
1969, 1970, 1971, 1973 (twice), 1974
Published in Penguin Books 1976
Reprinted 1977, 1978, 1983, 1986

ISBN 014 058.593 1

Library of Congress catalog card number: 37-28693

Printed in the United States of America by
The Murray Printing Co., Westford, Massachusetts
Set in Cloister Oldstyle

CHAMBER

MUSIC

I

Strings in the earth and air
   Make music sweet;
Strings by the river where
   The willows meet.

There's music along the river
   For Love wanders there,
Pale flowers on his mantle,
   Dark leaves on his hair.

All softly playing,
   With head to the music bent,
And fingers straying
   Upon an instrument.

II

The twilight turns from amethyst
 To deep and deeper blue,
The lamp fills with a pale green glow
 The trees of the avenue.

The old piano plays an air,
 Sedate and slow and gay;
She bends upon the yellow keys,
 Her head inclines this way.

Shy thoughts and grave wide eyes and hands
 That wander as they list—
The twilight turns to darker blue
 With lights of amethyst.

III

At that hour when all things have repose,
   O lonely watcher of the skies,
   Do you hear the night wind and the sighs
Of harps playing unto Love to unclose
   The pale gates of sunrise?

When all things repose do you alone
   Awake to hear the sweet harps play
   To Love before him on his way,
And the night wind answering in antiphon
   Till night is overgone?

Play on, invisible harps, unto Love,
   Whose way in heaven is aglow
   At that hour when soft lights come and go,
Soft sweet music in the air above
   And in the earth below.

IV

When the shy star goes forth in heaven
    All maidenly, disconsolate,
Hear you amid the drowsy even
    One who is singing by your gate.
His song is softer than the dew
    And he is come to visit you.

O bend no more in revery
    When he at eventide is calling,
Nor muse: Who may this singer be
    Whose song about my heart is falling?
Know you by this, the lover's chant,
    'Tis I that am your visitant.

V

Lean out of the window,
   Goldenhair,
I heard you singing
   A merry air.

My book was closed;
   I read no more,
Watching the fire dance
   On the floor.

I have left my book,
   I have left my room,
For I heard you singing
   Through the gloom.

Singing and singing
   A merry air,
Lean out of the window,
   Goldenhair.

VI

I would in that sweet bosom be
   (O sweet it is and fair it is!)
Where no rude wind might visit me.
   Because of sad austerities
I would in that sweet bosom be.

I would be ever in that heart
   (O soft I knock and soft entreat her!)
Where only peace might be my part.
   Austerities were all the sweeter
So I were ever in that heart.

VII

My love is in a light attire
    Among the apple-trees,
Where the gay winds do most desire
    To run in companies.

There, where the gay winds stay to woo
    The young leaves as they pass,
My love goes slowly, bending to
    Her shadow on the grass;

And where the sky's a pale blue cup
    Over the laughing land,
My love goes lightly, holding up
    Her dress with dainty hand.

VIII

Who goes amid the green wood
    With springtide all adorning her?
Who goes amid the merry green wood
    To make it merrier?

Who passes in the sunlight
    By ways that know the light footfall?
Who passes in the sweet sunlight
    With mien so virginal?

The ways of all the woodland
    Gleam with a soft and golden fire—
For whom does all the sunny woodland
    Carry so brave attire?

O, it is for my true love
    The woods their rich apparel wear—
O, it is for my own true love,
    That is so young and fair.

IX

Winds of May, that dance on the sea,
Dancing a ring-around in glee
From furrow to furrow, while overhead
The foam flies up to be garlanded,
In silvery arches spanning the air,
Saw you my true love anywhere?
  Welladay! Welladay!
  For the winds of May!
  Love is unhappy when love is away!

X

Bright cap and streamers,
  He sings in the hollow:
  Come follow, come follow,
  All you that love.
Leave dreams to the dreamers
  That will not after,
  That song and laughter
  Do nothing move.

With ribbons streaming
  He sings the bolder;
  In troop at his shoulder
  The wild bees hum.
And the time of dreaming
  Dreams is over—
  As lover to lover,
  Sweetheart, I come.

XI

Bid adieu, adieu, adieu,
   Bid adieu to girlish days,
Happy Love is come to woo
   Thee and woo thy girlish ways—
The zone that doth become thee fair,
The snood upon thy yellow hair.

When thou hast heard his name upon
   The bugles of the cherubim
Begin thou softly to unzone
   Thy girlish bosom unto him
And softly to undo the snood
That is the sign of maidenhood.

XII

What counsel has the hooded moon
　　Put in thy heart, my shyly sweet,
Of Love in ancient plenilune,
　　Glory and stars beneath his feet—
A sage that is but kith and kin
With the comedian Capuchin?

Believe me rather that am wise
　　In disregard of the divine,
A glory kindles in those eyes,
　　Trembles to starlight. Mine, O Mine!
No more be tears in moon or mist
For thee, sweet sentimentalist.

XIII

Go seek her out all courteously,
   And say I come,
Wind of spices whose song is ever
   Epithalamium.
O, hurry over the dark lands
   And run upon the sea
For seas and land shall not divide us
   My love and me.

Now, wind, of your good courtesy
   I pray you go,
And come into her little garden
   And sing at her window;
Singing: The bridal wind is blowing
   For Love is at his noon;
And soon will your true love be with you,
   Soon, O soon.

XIV

My dove, my beautiful one,
   Arise, arise!
   The night-dew lies
Upon my lips and eyes.

The odorous winds are weaving
   A music of sighs:
   Arise, arise,
My dove, my beautiful one!

I wait by the cedar tree,
   My sister, my love.
   White breast of the dove,
My breast shall be your bed.

The pale dew lies
   Like a veil on my head.
   My fair one, my fair dove,
Arise, arise!

XV

From dewy dreams, my soul, arise,
  From love's deep slumber and from death,
For lo! the trees are full of sighs
  Whose leaves the morn admonisheth.

Eastward the gradual dawn prevails
  Where softly-burning fires appear,
Making to tremble all those veils
  Of grey and golden gossamer.

While sweetly, gently, secretly,
  The flowery bells of morn are stirred
And the wise choirs of faery
  Begin (innumerous!) to be heard.

XVI

O cool is the valley now
   And there, love, will we go
For many a choir is singing now
   Where Love did sometime go.
And hear you not the thrushes calling,
   Calling us away?
O cool and pleasant is the valley
   And there, love, will we stay.

XVII

Because your voice was at my side
    I gave him pain,
Because within my hand I held
    Your hand again.

There is no word nor any sign
    Can make amend—
He is a stranger to me now
    Who was my friend.

XVIII

O Sweetheart, hear you
   Your lover's tale;
A man shall have sorrow
   When friends him fail.

For he shall know then
   Friends be untrue
And a little ashes
   Their words come to.

But one unto him
   Will softly move
And softly woo him
   In ways of love.

His hand is under
   Her smooth round breast;
So he who has sorrow
   Shall have rest.

XIX

Be not sad because all men
   Prefer a lying clamour before you:
Sweetheart, be at peace again—
   Can they dishonour you?

They are sadder than all tears;
   Their lives ascend as a continual sigh.
Proudly answer to their tears:
   As they deny, deny.

XX

In the dark pine-wood
   I would we lay,
In deep cool shadow
   At noon of day.

How sweet to lie there,
   Sweet to kiss,
Where the great pine-forest
   Enaisled is!

Thy kiss descending
   Sweeter were
With a soft tumult
   Of thy hair.

O, unto the pine-wood
   At noon of day
Come with me now,
   Sweet love, away.

XXI

He who hath glory lost, nor hath
    Found any soul to fellow his,
Among his foes in scorn and wrath
    Holding to ancient nobleness,
That high unconsortable one —
His love is his companion.

XXII

Of that so sweet imprisonment
　　My soul, dearest, is fain—
Soft arms that woo me to relent
　　And woo me to detain.
Ah, could they ever hold me there
Gladly were I a prisoner!

Dearest, through interwoven arms
　　By love made tremulous,
That night allures me where alarms
　　Nowise may trouble us;
But sleep to dreamier sleep be wed
Where soul with soul lies prisoned.

XXIII

This heart that flutters near my heart
   My hope and all my riches is,
Unhappy when we draw apart
   And happy between kiss and kiss;
My hope and all my riches—yes!—
And all my happiness.

For there, as in some mossy nest
   The wrens will divers treasures keep,
I laid those treasures I possessed
   Ere that mine eyes had learned to weep.
Shall we not be as wise as they
Though love live but a day?

XXIV

Silently she's combing,
    Combing her long hair,
Silently and graciously,
    With many a pretty air.

The sun is in the willow leaves
    And on the dappled grass,
And still she's combing her long hair
    Before the looking-glass.

I pray you, cease to comb out,
    Comb out your long hair,
For I have heard of witchery
    Under a pretty air,

That makes as one thing to the lover
    Staying and going hence,
All fair, with many a pretty air
    And many a negligence.

XXV

Lightly come or lightly go:
　　Though thy heart presage thee woe,
Vales and many a wasted sun,
　　Oread, let thy laughter run,
Till the irreverent mountain air
Ripple all thy flying hair.

Lightly, lightly — ever so:
　　Clouds that wrap the vales below
At the hour of evenstar
　　Lowliest attendants are;
Love and laughter song-confessed
When the heart is heaviest.

XXVI

Thou leanest to the shell of night,
    Dear lady, a divining ear.
In that soft choiring of delight
    What sound hath made thy heart to fear?
Seemed it of rivers rushing forth
From the grey deserts of the north?

    That mood of thine, O timorous,
Is his, if thou but scan it well,
    Who a mad tale bequeaths to us
At ghosting hour conjurable—
    And all for some strange name he read
    In Purchas or in Holinshed.

XXVII

Though I thy Mithridates were,
   Framed to defy the poison-dart.
Yet must thou fold me unaware
   To know the rapture of thy heart,
And I but render and confess
The malice of thy tenderness.

For elegant and antique phrase,
   Dearest, my lips wax all too wise;
Nor have I known a love whose praise
   Our piping poets solemnize,
Neither a love where may not be
Ever so little falsity.

XXVIII

Gentle lady, do not sing
    Sad songs about the end of love;
Lay aside sadness and sing
    How love that passes is enough.

Sing about the long deep sleep
    Of lovers that are dead, and how
In the grave all love shall sleep:
    Love is aweary now.

XXIX

Dear heart, why will you use me so?
  Dear eyes that gently me upbraid,
Still are you beautiful—but O,
  How is your beauty raimented!

Through the clear mirror of your eyes,
  Through the soft cry of kiss to kiss,
Desolate winds assail with cries
  The shadowy garden where love is.

And soon shall love dissolved be
  When over us the wild winds blow—
But you, dear love, too dear to me,
  Alas! why will you use me so?

XXX

Love came to us in time gone by
    When one at twilight shyly played
And one in fear was standing nigh—
    For Love at first is all afraid.

We were grave lovers. Love is past
    That had his sweet hours many a one;
Welcome to us now at the last
    The ways that we shall go upon.

XXXI

O, it was out by Donnycarney
    When the bat flew from tree to tree
My love and I did walk together;
    And sweet were the words she said to me.

Along with us the summer wind
    Went murmuring—O, happily!—
But softer than the breath of summer
    Was the kiss she gave to me.

XXXII

Rain has fallen all the day.
  O come among the laden trees:
The leaves lie thick upon the way
  Of memories.

Staying a little by the way
  Of memories shall we depart.
Come, my beloved, where I may
  Speak to your heart.

XXXIII

Now, O now, in this brown land
    Where Love did so sweet music make
We two shall wander, hand in hand,
    Forbearing for old friendship' sake,
Nor grieve because our love was gay
Which now is ended in this way.

A rogue in red and yellow dress
    Is knocking, knocking at the tree;
And all around our loneliness
    The wind is whistling merrily.
The leaves—they do not sigh at all
When the year takes them in the fall.

Now, O now, we hear no more
    The villanelle and roundelay!
Yet will we kiss, sweetheart, before
    We take sad leave at close of day.
Grieve not, sweetheart, for anything—
The year, the year is gathering.

XXXIV

Sleep now, O sleep now,
   O you unquiet heart!
A voice crying "Sleep now"
   Is heard in my heart.

The voice of the winter
   Is heard at the door.
O sleep, for the winter
   Is crying "Sleep no more."

My kiss will give peace now
   And quiet to your heart—
Sleep on in peace now,
   O you unquiet heart!

XXXV

All day I hear the noise of waters
    Making moan,
Sad as the sea-bird is, when going
    Forth alone,
He hears the winds cry to the waters'
    Monotone.

The grey winds, the cold winds are blowing
    Where I go.
I hear the noise of many waters
    Far below.
All day, all night, I hear them flowing
    To and fro.

XXXVI

I hear an army charging upon the land,
    And the thunder of horses plunging, foam about
        their knees:
Arrogant, in black armour, behind them stand,
    Disdaining the reins, with fluttering whips, the
        charioteers.

They cry unto the night their battle-name:
    I moan in sleep when I hear afar their whirling
        laughter.
They cleave the gloom of dreams, a blinding flame,
    Clanging, clanging upon the heart as upon an
        anvil.

They come shaking in triumph their long, green
        hair:
    They come out of the sea and run shouting by
        the shore.
My heart, have you no wisdom thus to despair?
    My love, my love, my love, why have you left
        me alone?

POMES

PENYEACH

TILLY

He travels after a winter sun,
Urging the cattle along a cold red road,
Calling to them, a voice they know,
He drives his beasts above Cabra.

The voice tells them home is warm.
They moo and make brute music with their hoofs.
He drives them with a flowering branch before
    him,
Smoke pluming their foreheads.

Boor, bond of the herd,
Tonight stretch full by the fire!
I bleed by the black stream
For my torn bough!

WATCHING THE NEEDLEBOATS
AT SAN SABBA

I heard their young hearts crying
Loveward above the glancing oar
And heard the prairie grasses sighing:
No more, return no more!

O hearts, O sighing grasses,
Vainly your loveblown bannerets mourn!
No more will the wild wind that passes
Return, no more return.

A FLOWER GIVEN TO MY
DAUGHTER

Frail the white rose and frail are
Her hands that gave
Whose soul is sere and paler
Than time's wan wave.

Rosefrail and fair—yet frailest
A wonder wild
In gentle eyes thou veilest,
My blueveined child.

SHE WEEPS OVER RAHOON

Rain on Rahoon falls softly, softly falling,
Where my dark lover lies.
Sad is his voice that calls me, sadly calling,
At grey moonrise.

Love, hear thou
How soft, how sad his voice is ever calling,
Ever unanswered and the dark rain falling,
Then as now.

Dark too our hearts, O love, shall lie and cold
As his sad heart has lain
Under the moongrey nettles, the black mould
And muttering rain.

TUTTO È SCIOLTO

A birdless heaven, seadusk, one lone star
Piercing the west,
As thou, fond heart, love's time, so faint, so far,
Rememberest.

The clear young eyes' soft look, the candid brow,
The fragrant hair,
Falling as through the silence falleth now
Dusk of the air.

Why then, remembering those shy
Sweet lures, repine
When the dear love she yielded with a sigh
Was all but thine?

ON THE BEACH AT FONTANA

Wind whines and whines the shingle,
The crazy pierstakes groan;
A senile sea numbers each single
Slimesilvered stone.

From whining wind and colder
Grey sea I wrap him warm
And touch his trembling fineboned shoulder
And boyish arm.

Around us fear, descending
Darkness of fear above
And in my heart how deep unending
Ache of love!

SIMPLES

O bella bionda,
Sei come l'onda!

Of cool sweet dew and radiance mild
The moon a web of silence weaves
In the still garden where a child
Gathers the simple salad leaves.

A moondew stars her hanging hair
And moonlight kisses her young brow
And, gathering, she sings an air:
Fair as the wave is, fair, art thou!

Be mine, I pray, a waxen ear
To shield me from her childish croon
And mine a shielded heart for her
Who gathers simples of the moon.

FLOOD

Goldbrown upon the sated flood
The rockvine clusters lift and sway.
Vast wings above the lambent waters brood
Of sullen day.

A waste of waters ruthlessly
Sways and uplifts its weedy mane
Where brooding day stares down upon the sea
In dull disdain.

Uplift and sway, O golden vine,
Your clustered fruits to love's full flood,
Lambent and vast and ruthless as is thine
Incertitude!

NIGHTPIECE

Gaunt in gloom,
The pale stars their torches,
Enshrouded, wave.
Ghostfires from heaven's far verges faint illume,
Arches on soaring arches,
Night's sindark nave.

Seraphim,
The lost hosts awaken
To service till
In moonless gloom each lapses muted, dim,
Raised when she has and shaken
Her thurible.

And long and loud,
To night's nave upsoaring,
A starknell tolls
As the bleak incense surges, cloud on cloud,
Voidward from the adoring
Waste of souls.

ALONE

The moon's greygolden meshes make
All night a veil,
The shorelamps in the sleeping lake
Laburnum tendrils trail.

The sly reeds whisper to the night
A name—her name—
And all my soul is a delight,
A swoon of shame.

A MEMORY OF THE PLAYERS IN
A MIRROR AT MIDNIGHT

They mouth love's language. Gnash
The thirteen teeth
Your lean jaws grin with. Lash
Your itch and quailing, nude greed of the flesh.
Love's breath in you is stale, worded or sung,
As sour as cat's breath,
Harsh of tongue.

This grey that stares
Lies not, stark skin and bone.
Leave greasy lips their kissing. None
Will choose her what you see to mouth upon.
Dire hunger holds his hour.
Pluck forth your heart, saltblood, a fruit of
    tears.
Pluck and devour!

BAHNHOFSTRASSE

The eyes that mock me sign the way
Whereto I pass at eve of day,

Grey way whose violet signals are
The trysting and the twining star.

Ah star of evil! star of pain!
Highhearted youth comes not again

Nor old heart's wisdom yet to know
The signs that mock me as I go.

A PRAYER

Again!
Come, give, yield all your strength to me!
From far a low word breathes on the breaking brain
Its cruel calm, submission's misery,
Gentling her awe as to a soul predestined.
Cease, silent love! My doom!

Blind me with your dark nearness, O have mercy,
     beloved enemy of my will!
I dare not withstand the cold touch that I dread.
Draw from me still
My slow life! Bend deeper on me, threatening head,
Proud by my downfall, remembering, pitying
Him who is, him who was!

Again!
Together, folded by the night, they lay on earth.
     I hear
From far her low word breathe on my breaking
     brain.
Come! I yield. Bend deeper upon me! I am here.
Subduer, do not leave me! Only joy, only anguish,
Take me, save me, soothe me, O spare me!

ECCE PUER

ECCE PUER

Of the dark past
A child is born
With joy and grief
My heart is torn

Calm in his cradle
The living lies.
May love and mercy
Unclose his eyes!

Young life is breathed
On the glass;
The world that was not
Comes to pass.

A child is sleeping:
An old man gone.
O, father forsaken,
Forgive your son!